Digby
to the rescue

By Alan Aburrow-Newman

Illustrated by Gill Guile

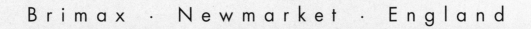
Brimax · Newmarket · England

ISBN 1 85854 638 9
Published by Brimax Books Ltd, Newmarket, England, CB8 7AU, 1997
Printed in Dubai.

Digby
the
Dinosaur

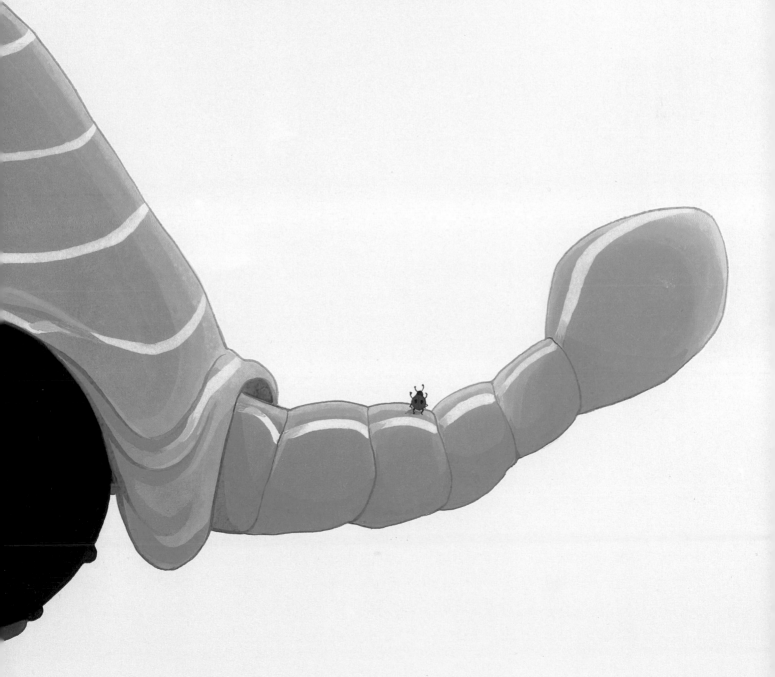

Very early one Saturday morning, Big Bill the driver arrived at Digby's garage. Over his shoulder and around his neck was a long hose. It was coiled so high, Digby could just see the top of Big Bill's cap! He had a scrubbing brush in one hand, and a bucket filled with sponges and soap in the other. Cleaning rags stuck out of every pocket.

"We have an important job to do today," said Big Bill. "You must look as smart as the day you arrived at the garage. At the moment you look like the world's biggest mud pie!"

Digby felt nervous. He liked being muddy, and he had a horrible feeling that something wet and soapy was about to happen.

Digby had never had a bath quite like it! Buckets of water were thrown over him. He was brushed and scrubbed and squirted so hard with the hose, that lumps of mud went flying in all directions. The garage floor looked like a muddy pond. At last Digby began to look like a digger again.

"Where are we going?" asked Digby, wriggling as his tummy was squirted with water.

"If I tell you, it will spoil the surprise," said Big Bill. "And the sooner you keep still, the sooner you will find out!"

Washed and polished, Digby really did look as good as new. His bright yellow paintwork was gleaming; his glass was glittering; his wheels were the brightest yellow. "Oh! Please tell me," said Digby. "Where are we going?"

"You will just have to wait and see," said Big Bill. "Today we are going somewhere very special." Big Bill changed his boots for shiny shoes and climbed into his seat in the cab.

"Off we go then," he said happily as he started Digby's engine.

Driving through the town, Digby passed lots of places that *he* thought were special. First of all there was the lemonade factory, where he had made the new truck parking lot.

Then there was the playground, where he had put the new swings and slides.

14

There was the swimming pool that he had dug all on his own.

And there was the park where he had made the flower beds, and a pond with a fountain for the goldfish. But they didn't stop at any of these places.

"We are almost there now," said Big Bill. "Close your eyes and I will tell you when to open them. And make sure you don't peek!"
Digby was just about to have a quick peek, when he heard lots of children calling his name.
"Hoorah for Digby!" they were shouting.

Digby opened his eyes. He was at the school. "What am I doing here? Am I making a new playground or helping to plant some big trees?" "No!" shouted the children. "We are going to dress you up for the carnival!" They were so excited, they skipped and danced around Digby until he began to feel dizzy.

The children began dressing Digby up. They put bright green blankets over his cab and wrapped green cloth around his digging arm.

"What am I going to be in the carnival?" Digby asked Thomas, who was painting him with wiggly, yellow stripes.

"Wait and see," said Thomas.

18

"What are you dressing me up as?" Digby asked Harriet and Laura. They were sticking big, white cardboard teeth onto his front digging bucket.

"Stop asking questions," said Harriet.
"You are not supposed to find out until we've finished," said Laura.

"Joshua, will you tell me what I look like?" Digby said to the little boy painting two red eyes next to the big teeth.
"I can't! It's a secret!" Joshua whispered back.

"Please tell me! *Please!*" said Digby. "A secret is no fun when I am the only one who doesn't know what the secret is!"

"They are nearly finished," said Big Bill. He was helping to put some big rubber feet onto Digby's wheels. "Now there is only the tail to go!"

When the children had finished wrapping and sticking and painting and fixing, they all stood in a big circle around Digby. He had never seen so many smiling faces.

"You are the biggest and best in the world," the children shouted.

"We've made you green with yellow stripes, with bright, red eyes, huge teeth, big feet and a long tail. You look at least a million years old. Guess what you are, Digby?"

Digby thought hard, but he couldn't think of a single thing that was green with yellow stripes, red eyes, huge teeth, big feet and a long tail. "I give up," he said at last. "Now PLEASE tell me what I am!"

"You are a dinosaur!" the children cried. "A huge green and yellow dinosaur!"

Digby saw his reflection in the school window. He really *did* look like a dinosaur. His front bucket was a big, square head which he could lift up as high as a house. He had a big mouth and sharp, pointed teeth. His cab was a lumpy, humpy back and he had a long, snaky tail that he could swish from side to side. The rubber feet were best of all. They slapped and flopped as his wheels went round, making noises just like a real dinosaur walking in puddles.

24

"I am a **diggersaurus**!" said Digby. "The strangest dinosaur of all!"

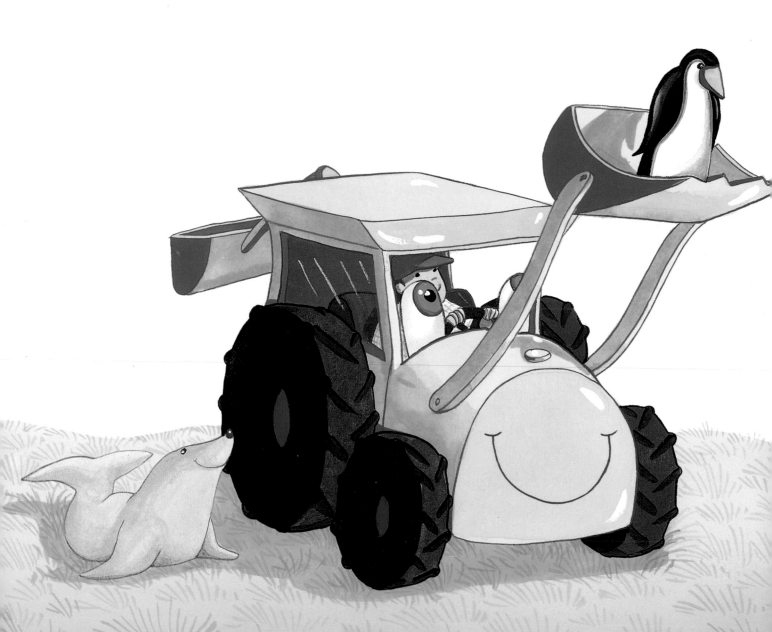

Digby

Helps at the Zoo

It was a hot, sunny day. Digby was helping to build a new playground for the gorillas at the zoo. It had to be strong, because the gorillas had broken the last one. The new one had stronger poles for climbing on, thicker rope for swinging from and tougher nets for jumping into.

The gorillas were pleased with their new playground. Just to make sure that Digby had made a good job of everything, they decided to give it their own special test. Wallop, the biggest gorilla, jumped up and down on the bridge. Another gorilla did a forward roll down the slide. Five others tugged at the same knotted rope. They all crashed and banged, but nothing was broken. Digby was very pleased.

"No matter how hard they try, I don't think the gorillas will wreck this playground," he said.

Digby noticed Ernie and Edna the hippos in the next paddock. They looked very grumpy. They were standing in a dirty pit, puffing and snorting, and blowing dust into the air. Larry, the head keeper, was sitting on the fence spraying them with water from a hose.

"Oh dear," said Digby. "Are you going to give them a bath?"
Larry looked hot and bothered, too.
"No, I'm just trying to cool them down," he said. "They are too hot,
and the sun has dried up the mud in their hollow."
"Well, if Ernie and Edna get much hotter, they will shrivel up like giant
raisins!" said Digby.
"They need lots of mud to cool down in," said Larry.

"Leave this to me," said Digby. "Come on, Big Bill," said Digby to his driver.
"Let's visit the sea-lions."

It was feeding time at the sea-lions' pool. Their keeper was throwing them fish to eat and a crowd of children was cheering as the sea-lions leaped out of the water.

"The sea-lions will be too busy to notice what I'm doing," said Digby.
"What are you planning?" asked Big Bill. "I hope you're not going to get us into trouble."
"I thought we could *borrow* some of the sea-lions' water, and use it to make a muddy pond for the hippos," said Digby.
"What a good idea!" said Big Bill excitedly. "But how are we going to get the water back to the hippo paddock?"
"That's easy," said Digby.

Digby plunged his front bucket into the sea-lions' pool, and scooped up enough water to fill twenty bath-tubs. He was just about to go back to the hippo paddock when a sea-lion peered over the edge of the bucket.

"Oh dear! I've kidnapped a sea-lion," chuckled Digby. "You had better get out of there, unless you want to share a mud-hole with two hippos!" The sea-lion leaped out of the bucket, and dived back into his pool.

When he arrived back at the hippos' paddock, Digby dumped the water with such a splash, that it washed Larry off the fence. Ernie and Edna cheered up when they saw the water, but it still wasn't mud. They wanted mud as gooey as a double-thick milkshake, so they could roll around until they looked like two chocolate hippos.

"I'll show you how to make mud!" said Digby.

Making mud was the best thing about being a digger. After a few minutes of churning and turning, the water had become a lovely deep, sticky mud that almost covered Digby's wheels.

"There you are," said Digby to Ernie and Edna, as he finally backed out of the pit. "First class mud; smooth and cool, and not a single lump!"
Ernie and Edna very slowly walked into the cool, chocolate-brown goo. They sank down in it until all that could be seen was their sleepy eyes and blissful smiles.

"Hmm," said Digby. "I wouldn't mind being a hippo myself."
Feeling very pleased with themselves, Digby and Big Bill began to head
back to the garage. Suddenly Larry, who was still very wet, signalled for
Digby to stop.

"Will you give me a ride to the giraffes' enclosure?" Larry asked. "Patches has a problem."

When they arrived, Digby could see that Patches really *did* have a problem. For a giraffe, a problem couldn't get much bigger, or longer, than a stiff neck!

Because Patches couldn't reach down to his food, he hadn't been able to eat all day. Kevin, his keeper, was trying to feed Patches by throwing fruit and vegetables for him to catch in his mouth. Kevin wasn't very good at throwing and Patches wasn't very good at catching. All they had managed to do was wedge a melon between Patches' horns!

"I can help," said Digby. "If you load Patches' dinner into my bucket, I can lift it up to him."

Larry, Big Bill and Kevin filled Digby's bucket with fruit and vegetables, a bale of hay and a big tub of water.

"Here comes dinner!" called Digby to Patches, and he stretched up as high as he could, so Patches could eat without bending down.

Patches couldn't decide what to eat first, so he ate a big, juicy apple while he thought about it. Eventually he decided to eat the carrots first, as he liked carrots more than anything!

After a long day standing up - and after such a fine supper, too -
Patches wished that he could lay down to sleep. Then Digby started
to yawn as well. After such a busy day, he could hardly keep his eyes
open. Big Bill piled a huge feather pillow into Digby's bucket and lifted
it up for Patches to rest his head on. Then, switching off Digby's
engine, Big Bill crept away.

Soon Patches and Digby were both fast asleep.

Digby
and the Big Flood

Digby was digging a trench along the edge of the road by the river. It had been raining hard and Big Bill had to get a pump to suck the water out of the trench. Digby liked working with the pump - it made a lovely slurping noise and poured muddy water over the road.

Digby noticed there was more and more water in the trench. The pump couldn't suck the water out fast enough.

"What's going on?" cried Digby. "We need another pump."

"I don't think it would help if we had ten pumps," said Big Bill. "Look! The river has burst its banks - the whole town will be flooded soon!"

Digby looked along the road that ran into town. The streets and gardens were disappearing under water.
"Come on, Big Bill," said Digby. "We must see if we can help!"

As they drove along the main street and into the middle of town, Digby and Big Bill saw people leaning out of windows, calling for help.
"The town is completely flooded," called Lenny the baker.
"And the telephones and electricity are cut off," said Maggie from the pizza house.

50

"We can't get any help!"
Just then, Digby saw Jimmy Seed's farm trailer in an alley.
"Don't worry, I have an idea," he said. "Let's hitch up that trailer, Big Bill,
then we can pick up all the stranded people."

With the trailer behind him, Digby drove slowly through the flooded streets. He stopped under windows so people could climb down into the trailer. At some houses, the windows were so high, Digby used his back arm like a slide so people could slide down to the trailer.

Mrs McKenzie at the pet store had her two goats, Clarence and Susan with her. They were bleating for help. Clarence was so nervous, he was eating a tablecloth.

"How can we all get down?" called Mrs McKenzie to Digby.
"Climb into my back bucket and I will lift you down into the trailer."
"But we can't all get into that little bucket," said Mrs McKenzie.
"There's Clarence, Susan and me, three parrots in cages, two rabbits, four kittens and a puppy!"

"You will have to take it in turns," said Digby. "Put all the animals in first."

Mrs McKenzie persuaded the two greedy goats to hop from the window by tossing a tasty-looking potted plant into the bucket. Then Mrs McKenzie carefully lifted the small animals and the parrots into Digby's bucket. Once the animals were safe, it was Mrs McKenzie's turn to ride in Digby's bucket. At last Digby called, "Hold on tight!" And with the trailer loaded with people and animals, he set off through the swirling water.

As they drove through the flooded town, Digby saw Pete the taxi driver. He seemed to be sitting *on* the water.

"That's very clever of you," called Digby. "You must be a very floaty sort of person to be able to sit *on* the water!"

"I'm not sitting on the water," replied Pete. "I'm sitting on the roof of my taxi! Have you any room for me in your trailer?"

"I'm sure we have space for a floaty taxi driver," said Digby with a smile.

Everyone squeezed up a little more to make room for Pete. Then off they went again, heading out of town towards the hills.

They were just passing the 'Supa Slick Oil Company' when Lenny the baker called out, "You had better get a move on, Digby. The water is coming into the trailer."

"I can't go any faster," puffed Digby. "It's really hard work pulling such a heavy trailer through this deep water."

"We need a boat," said Big Bill.

"Or we could be a boat," said Digby, as he watched a big, red oil barrel float past. Then he noticed more empty barrels bobbing around in the oil company yard. Digby had another idea.

"Come on, Big Bill," he said. "We need those oil barrels tied to me and the trailer!"

Big Bill climbed down into the water and caught hold of a barrel. He tied it tightly to Digby's front bucket with rope. Then helped by Lenny and Pete, Big Bill surrounded Digby with empty barrels. Then they collected more barrels and tied them to the trailer.

"We may be the strangest boat ever seen," said Digby, "but at least we should float if the water gets any deeper."

Digby and the trailer headed towards the bridge. Suddenly Digby stopped. He could see green hills and fields just across the river. "The bridge is under water," he said. "It might be unsafe to cross."

"We will have to try and drive over the bridge to check that it is safe," said Big Bill. "It might even be washed away in the middle."
They left the trailer tied to a tree so that it didn't float away. Then Digby and Big Bill drove slowly across the bridge.

62

"I hope these oil barrel floats work," said Digby.
Suddenly, Digby's big front wheels tipped off the edge of the broken bridge.
"Oh, no!" cried Digby. "Hold on, Big Bill!" and with a huge splash they disappeared under the water like a diving whale. Then Digby bounced off the river bed and began to float back to the surface! Whoosh!
He burst back into rainy sunshine.

Everyone on the trailer cheered as Digby bobbed along.

"These barrels may not be the best-looking water wings, but they certainly work," said Big Bill in relief, emptying water from his boots. "Oh, I knew they would," said Digby, who was secretly more relieved than Big Bill. "My ideas always work."

Spinning his rear wheels like a paddle steamer and using his back bucket as a rudder, Digby headed back to the trailer.
"Full steam ahead, Captain!" he called happily.
Digby towed everyone safely across the river.
"Who needs bridges!" he said cheerfully as he pulled his friends onto dry land.

Digby
the
Fire-Fighter

Digby had been working hard all morning, digging up the road through the forest. He was enjoying a rest while Big Bill, his driver, sat in the shade of a tree to eat his picnic lunch.

Suddenly a deer ran out of the forest. It leapt over the piles of stones and earth that Digby had left in the road, and ran off across the fields.

Then a rabbit followed the deer, and then a fox - until all sorts of birds and animals were rushing from the forest.

"That's very strange," said Digby. "I wonder what they are running away from?"

As Digby spoke, clouds of smoke came out of the forest.
"It's a forest fire!" shouted Digby. "Call the fire-fighters, Big Bill!"

"That won't do any good," said Big Bill, jumping up from his lunch.
"They can't get through because we've dug up the road!"
"Oh no!" said Digby. "Then we must do something. The fire is going
towards the town."

"We will have to make a gap in the trees so that the fire can't spread,"
said Big Bill. "You will have to be very brave."
"I'm not afraid," said Digby.

12

Big Bill tied a scarf around his face so the smoke wouldn't make him cough.

"Hey, what about me?" spluttered Digby. "I'm choking too!"

Big Bill tied the picnic cloth around Digby's face. "You look like a cowboy," he chuckled, "not a fire-fighter."

Then they bravely headed into the smoky forest.

Using his front bucket like a bulldozer, Digby cleared a wide track through the trees. It was even harder work than digging up the road. Digby could hear the flames crackling as the fire came closer, so he worked as fast as he could.

Digby and Big Bill finished just in time. The flames came right up to the edge of the track Digby had made. But they couldn't jump across the big gap to the trees on the other side. The fire quickly went out.

"Phew! That was close," said Digby as they reached the road again. "I'm glad I'm not a full time fire-fighter!"

Just then, Bobby Harvest the farmer pulled up in his truck. He looked very worried.

"There's a fire in the town!" shouted Bobby. "The fire-fighters cannot get to it because of road repairs. Their way is completely blocked."
"I'll come and see if I can help," said Digby.

Digby drove into town as fast as he could. In the middle of the town, an empty building was on fire. Smoke was pouring out of the windows and flames were flickering through the roof.

"It must have been a spark from the forest fire that started this," said Digby.

The fire was next door to 'Cool Joe's Ice-cream Store' - and it was so hot, the ice-cream was melting and running out through the door! There was a rainbow-river of strawberry surprise, chocolate-chip and tutti-frutti ice-cream running down the street!

"Now this is really serious!" said Digby.
"Just look at all that ice-cream!" said Big Bill in astonishment.
And then Cool Joe himself floated out of the doorway on a box.
He looked very unhappy. But the dogs and cats in the town were very
pleased. They lapped up the ice-cream as fast as they could.

The mayor had organised a line of men to throw buckets of water onto the flames. But the fire didn't seem to be going out.

"I have an idea," said Digby. "Let's get digging, Big Bill." They began to dig a hole outside the ice-cream store.

Deeper and deeper they dug until Big Bill asked, "How much further?" "Not far now," puffed Digby. "Almost there."

Suddenly Digby's bucket hit something hard in the bottom of the hole. "There it is, Big Bill," said Digby excitedly. It was the main water pipe.

Digby lifted his digging bucket high into the air and brought it down as hard as he could. There was a loud CLANG! Suddenly a huge fountain of water shot into the sky and rained down onto the fire. Soon the smoke turned to steam and the flames flickered out. Best of all, the ice-cream river slowed and stopped.

The children thought it was great fun dancing in the shower of water, and the sun made a real rainbow right across the town. Cool Joe was delighted that his store had been saved.

"There is just enough ice-cream left," he said to Big Bill. "So it's free ice-cream for everyone, thanks to Digby!"